I Can Draw THAT, TOO!

By Robert Pierce

Originally published as HOW TO DRAW PEOPLE and HOW TO DRAW CARTOONS

Copyright © 1999, 1985 by Robert Pierce. All rights reserved. Published by Grosset & Dunlap, Inc., a member of Penguin Putnam Books for Young Readers, New York. GROSSET & DUNLAP is a trademark of Grosset & Dunlap, Inc. BOOKS AND STUFF is a trademark of The Putnam & Grosset Group. Published simultaneously in Canada. Printed in the U.S.A. ISBN 0-448-42030-9   A B C D E F G H I J

I Can Draw THAT, TOO!

Learning to draw is fun! You will see how easy it is to draw people and all different kinds of things by following the step-by-step directions throughout this book. To begin, copy the stick figures on the next few pages. Then, as you go along, keep these important guidelines in mind:

- Try not to make your drawings too small—you can put more detail into a larger drawing.
- Use a soft pencil, crayon, or marker.
- To help you draw a special movement, act it out.
- When drawing facial expressions, look in a mirror and draw the way you <u>feel</u>—don't worry if it doesn't look exactly like you.
- Practice sketching things you see around you—the more you draw, the easier it will get.
- Use your imagination to make up even more people and scenes and stories!
- Do at least six drawings a day; you'll be surprised at the improvement. Practice makes perfect.

There you go. Now you too can be an artist!

START WITH A STICK FIGURE

STANDING

1 DRAW THE HEAD	2 ADD THE BODY	3 SHOULDERS AND HIPS
4 LEGS AND FEET	5 ARMS	6 READY TO GO

SITTING

1 DRAW A CHAIR	2 ADD THE HEAD	3 BODY
4 LEGS	5 ARMS	6 READING A BOOK

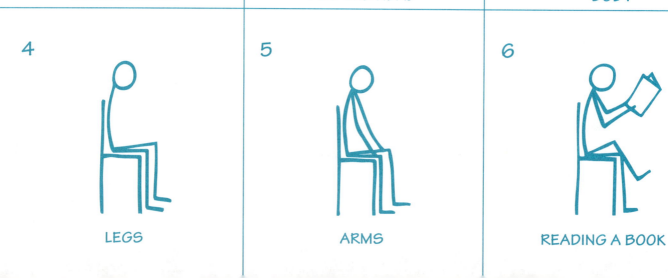

KNOCKOUT

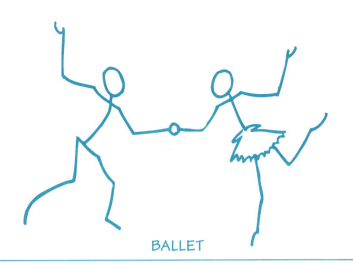

BALLET

COWBOY

SOCCER

TENNIS

SWING

SINGER

BULLFIGHTER

CARTOON STICK PEOPLE

CARTOON PEOPLE USUALLY HAVE LARGE HEADS	 SOME ARE STRONG	 SOME ARE PUNY
 TALL AND SKINNY	 SHAKY LEGS	 ALL DRESSED UP
 DIVER	 SLIPPERY ICE	 TRAPEZE ACROBAT
 FOOTBALL PLAYER	 MAJORETTE	 SUNBATHER

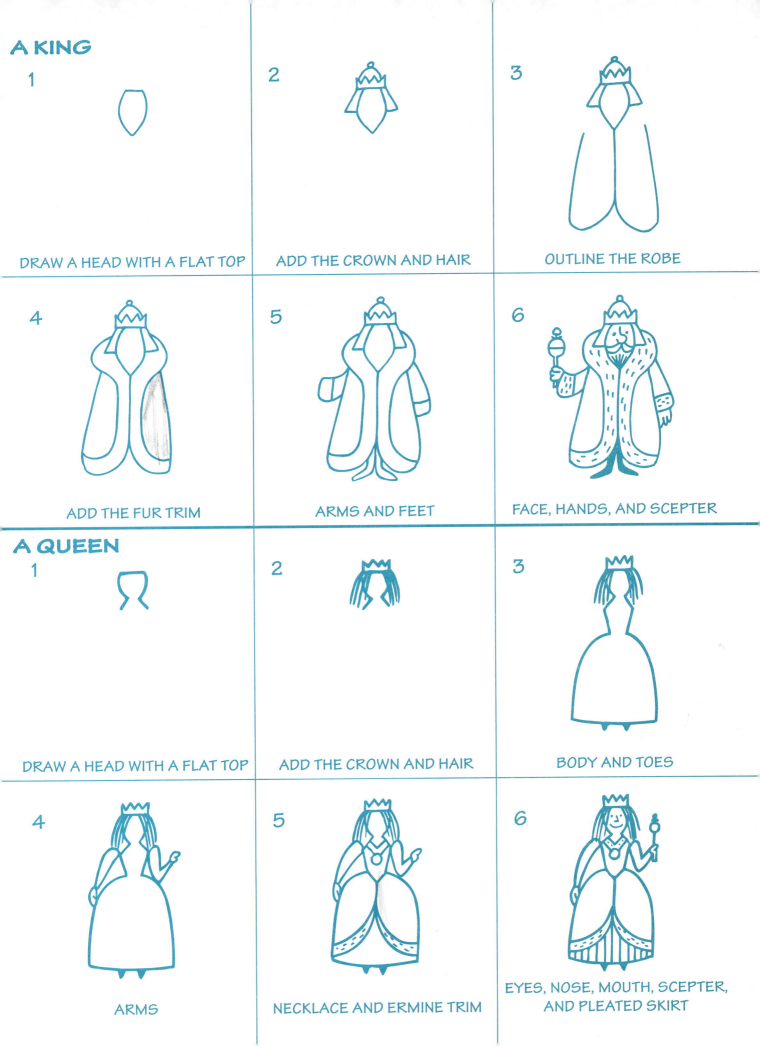

MAKING FACES

FRONT VIEW

1 DRAW THE HEAD

2 ADD A NOSE

3 EYES AND EYEBROWS

4 MOUTH

5 EARS

6 HAIR

SIDE VIEW

1 HEAD AND NOSE

2 EYE AND EYEBROW

3 MOUTH

4 EAR

5 MAN'S HAIR

6 WOMAN'S HAIR

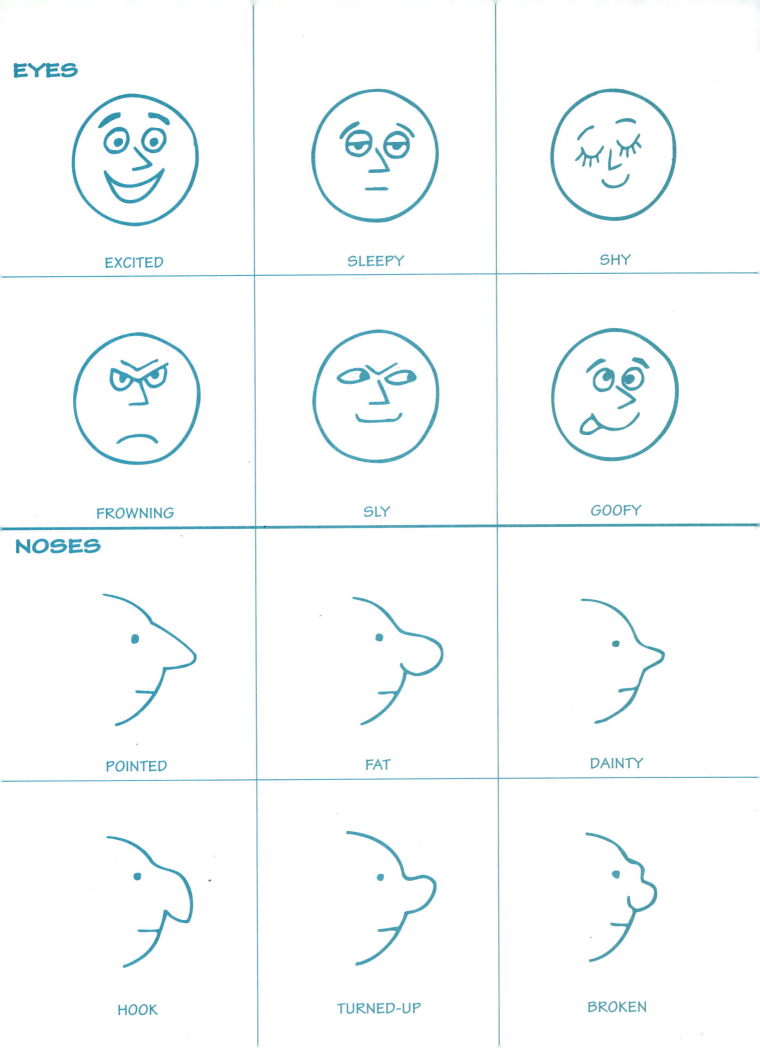

FEELINGS

HAPPY (front)	SAD (front)	WONDERING (front)
HAPPY (side)	SAD (side)	WONDERING (side)
DETERMINED (front)	WORRIED (front)	ANGRY (front)
DETERMINED (side)	WORRIED (side)	ANGRY (side)

DIFFERENT FACES

OLD MAN	YOUNG GIRL	POLICE OFFICER

NEIGHBOR	GOOD GUY	NICE WOMAN

SNEAKY	BORED	EAGER

TOUGH	STUCK-UP	THINKING

 FRECKLES	 SPACEY	 HUNGRY
 HELP!	 FEARFUL	 DOPEY

HAIR STYLES

 BANGS	 PIGTAILS	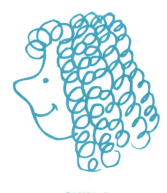 CURLS
 PONYTAIL	 BALD	 TOO MUCH HAIR

BODY SHAPES AND SIZES

ACTION LINES

SPEED LINES

FEELING DIZZY

STAGGERING

SEEING STARS

OVERHEATED

RAISING DUST

MUSCLE MOUSE

HAPPY HIPPO

PUZZLED TRAVELER

JUGGLER

WRONG ROAD

MUSIC FROM ABOVE

PRACTICE DRAWING EVERYTHING YOU SEE

HOME

DRAW YOUR HAND

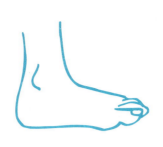
FOOT

BRUSH

CHAIR

SHIRT

TABLE

CUP AND SAUCER

SWEATER

PLANT

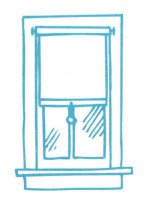
WINDOW

CAT

TREE

HATS

TOP HAT (front view)

TOP HAT (top view)

FLOWERED HAT

BASEBALL CAP

SKI CAP

STRAW HAT

SAILOR HAT

ROBIN HOOD HAT

10-GALLON HAT

WESTERN

HAT TOO BIG

HAT TOO SMALL

SHOES

WESTERN BOOT	HIKING BOOT	LOAFER

HIGH-HEELED SHOE	FUZZY SLIPPER	SNEAKER

ACCESSORIES

TIES	BOW TIES	GLASSES
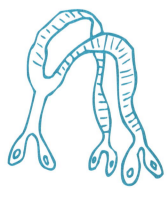		
SUSPENDERS	HOLEY SOCKS	PATCHES

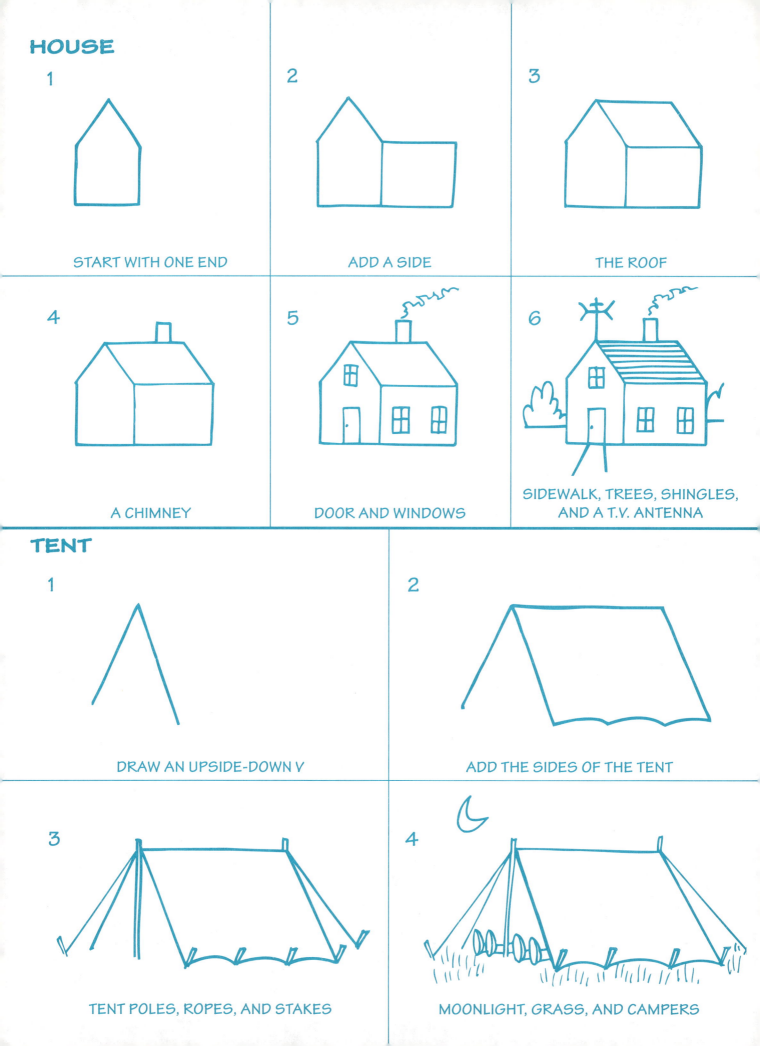

CITYSCAPE

1

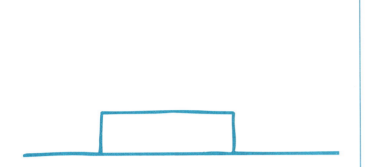

DRAW THE STREET LINE
AND A LOW BUILDING

2

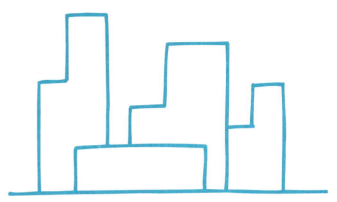

ADD SOME
TALLER BUILDINGS

3

ROOFS, CLOCK, AND FLAGPOLE

4

WINDOWS AND DOORS

CASTLE

1

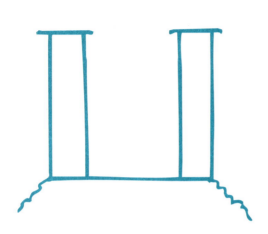

DRAW TWIN TOWERS ON A HILLTOP

2

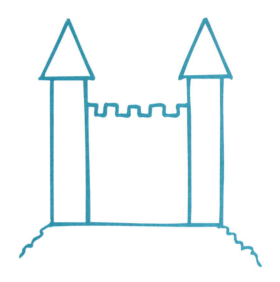

ADD TOWER ROOFS AND CASTLE WALL

3

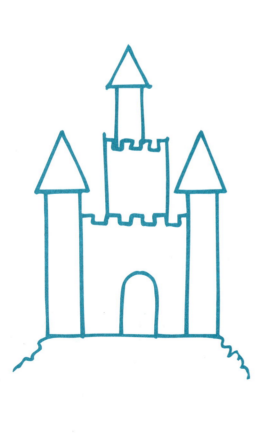

SECOND-STORY TOWER AND GATE

4

WINDOWS, FLAGS, AND ROAD

FENCES

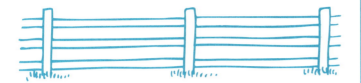
RAIL

PICKET

BARBED WIRE

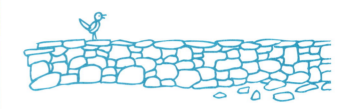
STONE

BOARD

BRICK WALL

TREES

SPRING

SUMMER

FALL

WINTER

PINE TREES

CHRISTMAS TREE

BUSHES AND GRASS

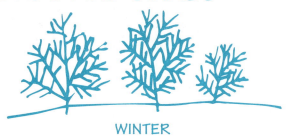
WINTER

LAWN

SUMMER

CLUMPS

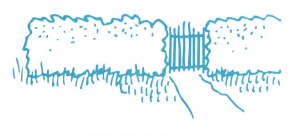
HEDGE AND GATE

TALL GRASS OR WEEDS

FLOWERS

TULIPS

DAISIES

ROSES

CATTAILS

DAFFODILS

SUNFLOWERS

JEEP

1 DRAW THE WHEELS

2 ADD RADIATOR AND BODY

3 ADD SEATS, WINDSHIELD, MUD GUARD, AND TIRE TREADS

4 ADD BUMPER, SPARE TIRE, AND STEERING WHEEL

LIMOUSINE

1 DRAW WHEELS ON A BASE LINE

2 ADD BUMPER, RADIATOR, AND HEADLIGHTS

3 ADD BODY, FENDERS, AND OTHER WHEELS

4 DOORS, WINDOWS, TAILLIGHT, AND HUBCAPS

WEATHER

1 WIND
2 RAIN
3 SNOW

LANDSCAPES

HILLS

MOUNTAINS AND TREES

SNOW-CAPPED MOUNTAINS

A CLIFF

COMIC ITEMS

NOISE WORDS

1	2	3
DRAW A HEAD, EARS, AND A HAT BRIM	ADD A SMASHED HAT	SHOULDERS

4	5	6
FLOWER POT	FLOWERS, FACE, AND NECKTIE	AND THE NOISE WORD

1	2	3
DRAW A HEAD	ADD A BODY AND A SECOND HEAD	ADD SECOND BODY AND ARMS

4	5	6
 SPOON AND MEDICINE	 EYES, EYEGLASSES, EAR, AND TONGUE	 AND THE NOISE WORD

MORE NOISE WORDS

DRAW PICTURES TO GO WITH THESE SOUNDS

BALLOONS

FOR CONVERSATION

FOR SILENT THOUGHTS

IDEAS

QUESTIONS

SURPRISES

AND WISHES

PUT THEM ALL TOGETHER!